D0601952

The Seattle School of Theology & Psychology
2501 Elliott Ave.
Seattle, WA 98121
theseattleschool.edu

When Emily Woke Up Angry

Riana Duncan

BARRON'S

New York

First edition for the United States published 1989
by Barron's Educational Series, Inc.
First published in 1989 by André Deutsch Limited, London, England

All inquiries should be addressed to:
Barron's Educational Series, Inc.
250 Wireless Boulevard
Hauppauge, New York 11788

International Standard Book No. 0–8120–5985–9

Library of Congress Catalog Card No. 88–22311

Library of Congress Cataloging-in-Publication Data

Duncan, Riana.
    When Emily woke up angry / Riana Duncan. - -1st ed.
        p. cm.
    Summary: Waking up in a bad mood. Emily initates the angry
movements of several animals until she meets a frog who jumps for
joy.
    ISBN 0–8120–5985–9
    [1. Anger - - Fiction.   2. Animals - - Fiction.]   I. Title.
PZ7.D913Wh 1989   88–22311
[E] - - dc19   CIP
                                                              AC
901 9 8 7 6 5 4 3 2 1

                    Printed in Portugal

One morning, Emily woke up angry.

"You've gotten out of bed on the wrong side,"
said her mother.
But Emily could only see one side of bed to get out of
and that made her even angrier.

She didn't want to wash her neck or behind her ears.
She didn't want to eat her breakfast.
"You had better run outside and cool off," said her mother,
"and come back when you've stopped being angry."

"What's the matter?" asked the cat.
"I'm angry," said Emily.
"When I'm angry," said the cat, "I arch my back
and puff up my tail and hiss."
So Emily arched her back and hissed,
but she didn't have a tail she could puff up
and she still felt angry.

"Why are you angry?" asked the dog.

"I don't know," said Emily. "I just am."

"When I'm angry," said the dog, "I growl. Like this."

So Emily growled too, but it only made her throat tickle and she still felt angry.

"What's wrong?" asked the hedgehog.
"I'm feeling angry today," said Emily.
"When I'm angry," said the hedgehog, "I roll myself
into a tight ball so that all my spikes stick out."
So Emily rolled herself into a tight ball,
but she had no spikes to stick out
and she didn't stop feeling angry.

"My, don't you look angry!" said the fly.
"When I'm angry, I buzz around and around in a great
big circle."
So Emily buzzed around and around in a great big circle
until she was dizzy, but she was still angry.

"Is anything the matter?" asked the horse.
"I'm angry today," said Emily.
"When I'm angry," said the horse, "I kick my legs."
Emily kicked her legs too,
but she still looked angry.

"Why do you look angry?" asked the gull.

"Just because," said Emily.

"When I'm angry," said the gull, "I flap my wings and make lots of noise."

So Emily waved her arms up and down and made lots and lots of noise, but she stayed angry.

"Whatever is wrong?" asked the rabbit.
"I'm angry," said Emily.
"I stamp my foot when I'm angry," said the rabbit.
And Emily stamped her foot too, but she didn't
stop being angry.

"I'm angry today," said Emily to the spider.
"If you must be angry," said the spider, "count to twenty-five.
That's what I do and when I'm REALLY angry,
I count all the way back again."
So Emily counted to twenty-five, but she didn't know
how to count all the way back, so she continued to
be angry.

"Why are you frowning?" asked the bull.

"I'm angry," said Emily.

"I paw the ground when I'm angry," said the bull,
"and I snort."

So Emily scraped at the ground with her shoe and snorted,
but she stayed angry.

"What's the matter?" asked the mouse.
"You're not angry, are you?
When I'm angry," the mouse went on, "I close my eyes
and try to think of nice things."
So Emily closed her eyes
and tried to think of nice things,
but she couldn't help thinking about being angry.

"You're not still angry, are you?" asked the frog.
"When I'm angry, I jump up and down and before I know
where I am, I'm jumping for joy!"
Emily jumped up and down, too.

Up and down she jumped, higher and higher.
Now, it is a very difficult thing to remember
to be angry when you're busy jumping up and down,
and soon Emily forgot all about being angry
and began to enjoy herself.

Then she felt hungry and went home to finish her breakfast.